EZRA THE BILLIONAIRE

SUITOR'S CROSSING: THE CALDWELLS #2

HALLIE BENNETT

Copyright © 2025 by Hallie Bennett

Searching for more from Suitor's Crossing?

Check out the *Mountain Men of Suitor's Crossing* series here[1]!

---

1. https://www.amazon.com/dp/B0BZ3F9GG4

PROLOGUE

LAUREN BILLINGSLEY

Agreeing to shoot a reality TV show is a bad idea. Cameras in your face. Manufactured drama for ratings. It's the absolute worst.

And then there's the fall out once the show airs for millions of people to laugh and snicker at your woes—a modern day Colosseum, where its gladiators aren't clad in leather and wielding swords, but lounging in sweats and crying into mimosas.

I knew before I signed the contract that it had the potential to blow up in my face, but sweet, *stupid* optimism blinded me. Along with love, or something that could've eventually turned into love if the explosion on *Harmony House* hadn't been fucking nuclear.

"Lauren, over here!" A paparazzi photog shouts, clamoring for a prime spot within the mosh pit of vultures staked in front of my hotel. I duck my head to avoid the flash of cameras and hug my oversized tote closer to my chest.

"Hunter and Mya's song 'My Lonesome Heart' is now number one on the pop charts. How jealous are you of their accomplishment?"

"No comment."

It's always *no comment*. Since the day I found my ex-boyfriend balls deep in an upcoming starlet, that's the only phrase I can legally say to the press.

The filming for our reality show, *Harmony House*, wrapped over a week ago, but the shocking reveal that my former boyfriend cheated on me with a fellow housemate aired for the entire world to see last night.

Hunter and I had co-written hundreds of songs before falling into a romantic relationship last year—a natural progression after spending hours together writing one romantic ballad after another. Which is why when he suggested we apply to join a show featuring songwriters and new singing talent living in a sort of creative mecca, I said 'yes.'

Boy, do I regret *that* decision.

Hopping into the rideshare whisking me away to the airport, I close the door on the frothing rabble outside the car and force a smile at the wide-eyed driver.

"Sorry for the chaos," I say, pulling the seatbelt across my chest and clicking it into place. My gaze stays fixed ahead rather than on the camera flashes piercing the windows.

"Should I know who you are?" The driver merges into traffic.

"Nope. These are just my fifteen minutes of fame before I'm forgotten." *Hopefully*. I mean who remembers reality TV participants? Unless they intend to turn their time in the limelight into brand deals as influencers, most fade into obscurity.

My only fear is that the drama of Hunter cheating on national television will make some sort of 'Top Ten' list of TV's most epic reveals or surprise twists. Then my humiliation will live on in infamy.

"What are you famous for?" the driver asks. Guess they're the curious, small-talk type.

Just my luck.

"I was on a show called *Harmony House*."

"Never heard of it."

"Thank god," I mutter under my breath. I'm praying no one in Suitor's Crossing has heard of it either, because I booked an extended stay at Hearthstone Lodge as part of my *Escape Hunter, That Damn Show, & the Paparazzi* plan.

The moment my phone began blowing up during last night's episode, I knew I was living on borrowed time in my quiet little bubble. Hunter's indiscretion made my admittedly boring storyline—writing songs, working with singers, and staying drama-free—suddenly newsworthy, and my poor apartment got bombarded by paps. Racing to a hotel with better security didn't help matters, so I took drastic measures and decided to flee the state.

Besides, a little R&R in the mountains sounds sublime, as long as I remain hidden from the public eye.

Surely, no one will follow me across the country, right?

CHAPTER ONE

EZRA CALDWELL

"Look out!" The shouted warning echoes in Hearthstone Lodge's atrium before a splash of cool liquid hits my head and shoulders, dousing me in something sweet and distinctly coffee-like. Ice cubes rain down and scatter across the marble tile as Keisha from the concierge desk hurries over.

"Are you alright?" She searches the upper levels of the lodge while speaking into a walkie-talkie. "Does someone have eyes on what happened?"

A couple of guests lean over the balconies to stare below, confusion rife on their faces until my narrowed gaze connects with violet eyes wide with guilt. Pointing at the woman, I tell Keisha, "*There*. Bring her to me. I'll be in my office drying off."

I shrug out of my suit jacket and tug at the soaking fabric clinging to my chest as I march out of the lobby, my shoes squeaking with each step.

This isn't the first time something has fallen from the tiered balconies surrounding the heart of the lodge. People are careless. They fumble cell phones, water bottles... Once, a social media influencer accidentally dropped an entire tray of sandwiches. I don't know what the hell they were trying to promote or how it happened, but a guest's golden retriever had been happy to gobble them up.

Most items land in the long planters strategically placed to avoid head-on collisions and massive legal fees, but there are a couple of unavoidable impact zones. Places where a guest has to stand just right from above, and an unlucky someone's timing becomes shit—like mine.

My younger sister Kennedy walks out of her office and abruptly stops. "What happened to you?"

"A cup of morning coffee, that's what." She follows me into my office down the hall and watches as I strip off the ruined shirt and replace it with an extra I keep in a desk drawer. Sometimes a late night turns into sleeping on the leather sofa in the corner, so it helps to keep spare clothing available for quick changes. My siblings joke about my overly prepared tendencies, but once again, it's proven to be necessary.

Kennedy tilts her head. "Did it explode in your face?" She gestures to the wet jacket and shirt, amusement hiding in the corners of her pressed lips.

"No, it fell from the damn sky." My fingers fight to push the tiny buttons through their holes on the fresh shirt as frustration quickens my pace. "Damn balconies. Damn clumsy-fingered, violet-eyed..." I continue to mutter under my breath when Keisha knocks on the doorframe with the culprit of my disastrous morning standing behind her.

"Lauren!" Kennedy greets the woman attempting to use Keisha as a barrier between us. "Is everything okay? Keisha, we've got it from here, thank you."

She nods, casts a sympathetic glance toward Lauren, then disappears.

"I spoke with security, and they assured me that you shouldn't have any more trouble with paparazzi while on the property. But if they're still hounding you..."

"No, no... That's not why I'm here." Lauren looks between me, Kennedy, and the discarded clothing hanging on the back of a chair before her gaze falls to my half-covered chest. A flush of scarlet rises to her cheeks as my dick swells with interest.

Dammit.

Who cares if there was a flare of attraction in her stare? Who cares if her rosy blush has me curious to know if it matches the color of her nipples?

I don't have time to lust after a guest.

She studiously refocuses on my sister. "There was an accident."

"That's putting it mildly," I grunt, determined to control the flame of desire threatening to spark free.

The last staff meeting replays in my mind as a distraction, and I recall the mention of increased security due to some minor celebrity arrival. *She* must be the celebrity. An actress? A model? Her pretty curves and wholesome features give off girl-next-door vibes—perfect for screen and print.

"Oh, no! You weren't the one who—"

"Yes, she was," I cut Kennedy off, snapping my collar into place after finishing with the damn shirt buttons. Though charcoal twill hides my bare chest from view, it doesn't quell the burn left from Lauren's brief show of interest.

"I'm so sorry. I saw someone with a camera and panicked." Lauren bites her lip, my eyes instinctively drawn to the pink plumpness before common sense takes over.

I don't need to be staring at Lauren's bow-shaped mouth. Or the way her breasts fill out that vee-neck sweater that shows just a hint of cleavage. No fucking way can I afford to be distracted by a beautiful woman when said beautiful woman is the reason I'm sticky, stinking of sugar and caffeine, and fighting an inappropriate hard-on.

And late for a meeting.

Plus, she's a *celebrity*. Probably an entitled diva.

My mind adds more fuel to the fire of annoyance in my gut and purposely ignores the lower stirring of attraction.

Kennedy's brow furrows. "Was it one of the gossip rag photographers? I'll let our head of security know."

"No, it wasn't. They didn't even have their camera pointed my way; it was hanging around their neck while they juggled a backpack and tumbler. I just..." She shrugged and sighed. "I wasn't thinking. That's how I bumped into the balcony railing and dropped my coffee."

A glance at my watch shows it's fifteen minutes after ten. This entire fiasco will have me running behind for the rest of the day.

Fuck.

I hate getting off schedule. That's my twin brother's specialty: going with the flow, pretending time has no meaning unless it involves an emergency for the fire department, then Beckett is all business.

After the quick swipe of a wet wipe—another item I keep on hand for emergencies—I toss the crumpled cloth and stare at Lauren.

I don't know why I had Keisha bring her here. It was obvious from her shock in the atrium that she didn't purposely drop her drink, so there's not much for me to do.

She's a lodge guest, and it wouldn't look good for the owner to scold her anyway.

"Next time, be more careful," I grumble, ushering both women out of my office. Hopefully, the photographer I'm meeting in one of the conference rooms won't be too pissed to be kept waiting for so long.

"Crap, don't you have that appointment with Jean Marcelle?" Kennedy asks as if reading my thoughts on my face.

"It started a quarter of an hour ago. Let's hope your tenuous connection to an influencer friend of Nora's is enough for him to overlook my tardiness."

Lauren stutter-steps and pitches forward on the carpet runner. Instinctively, my hands reach out to stop her fall—landing on her soft waist to squeeze gently—and a blast of something sweet tickles my nose.

Floral, not fruity.

Her shampoo?

"Sorry... *again*..." Lauren's grip on my arm tightens before she finds her footing and lets go. "Is Hearthstone Lodge a magnet for influencers? Or other high-profile guests? The lodge and town websites didn't mention being a hub like Aspen or Jackson Hole for celebrities."

"Don't worry; you won't run into anyone you know here. Nora Olson is a body-positive influencer, but she's also a local... *ish*. She lives in High Ridge," Kennedy explains. "The point is, one of her social media friends hosted an event at the lodge a few months ago, and over the course of organizing that event, we got on the subject of marketing and—" My sister stops to take a breath as we enter the atrium. She must realize she's running out of time to tell this story and jumps to the end. "She put me in contact with a photographer friend of hers. That's who Ezra is meeting with."

"Oh... Because you're the marketing director?" Curious violet eyes peek up at me. I didn't even know purple eyes were a real thing.

Are they real? They could be contacts.

Kennedy answers for me while I'm contemplating if Lauren is wearing contacts or not—something I shouldn't give a damn about.

"Ezra is my brother and manages Hearthstone for our family."

"I see. Now, I'm even sorrier for ruining your morning. I can pay for dry cleaning. Just send me the bill."

"Forget about it. Our laundry services will suffice. Ken, are you joining me?" The conference room is a few more steps. This little chat needs to end, so I can focus.

"Why don't we all go?" Kennedy snakes an arm through Lauren's to hold her in place.

"What?"

"Why?"

A mischievous grin forms as Kennedy drags her hostage forward while I tail behind them. "This isn't the paparazzi, Lauren. This is a professional whose purpose is to make Hearthstone Lodge look good to potential guests, and I think it'd be amazing if you posed for some shots. It'll be good for your image—representing a small-town resort—and we could use the heightened exposure for business."

My sister is talking out of her ass.

Never mind the bullshit about us fixing Lauren's public image, our finances are fine. We're not desperate for a celebrity endorsement to keep the lights on. Even if Hearthstone Lodge wasn't solvent on its own, I'm a fucking billionaire after starting my hedge fund over a decade ago.

"This is ridiculous. You're not—"

"Good morning, Mr. Marcelle. Apologies for our late arrival, but there was an accident that needed our immediate attention. Do you need anything before we get started? Water, coffee?" I swear Kennedy looks at me at that last part.

Ever since she fell in love with a military man she wrote letters to when he was thousands of miles away, she's been bolder, more outspoken—more like the rest of us Caldwells.

Which is good.

I'm happy to see my baby sister come out of her shell.

But damn... Does it have to mean bulldozing her way through my perfectly scheduled days?

And dragging the woman my body has an inconvenient attraction to along for the ride?

CHAPTER TWO

LAUREN

So much for a low profile.

First, I douse Hearthstone Lodge's handsome as sin manager and part-owner in my morning coffee—*way to go, Lauren*—then I agree to model for their marketing campaign.

What the actual hell?

I don't do press. I don't step out of the shadows in the background. The one fucking time I did is what landed me here in the first place! If I wanted to live in the spotlight, I'd sing my own songs instead of sticking with songwriting credits only.

"You. Stand over there." Jean Marcelle points to one of the water fountains delineating the four corners of the atrium. His huff of exasperation is the fifth so far, and it's only our first day of shooting.

After an awkward meeting with him, Kennedy, and Ezra, he'd reluctantly agreed to have me model. I say reluctantly because he couldn't refuse his clients' request outright, but judging by the unimpressed glare he shot my way, Jean Marcelle never deigned to photograph mere civilians. Supermodels only.

Like my companion, Jennifer Q.

No last name. Just Q.

Frankly, he doesn't seem particularly excited to shoot Hearthstone Lodge either—too rustic for his taste if I had to hazard a guess—so they must be paying him a buttload to secure his services.

"*Très magnifique*, Jen, darling," he coos, snapping pose after pose as Jennifer tilts her head or lifts a bony shoulder.

Très magnifique, Lauren, darling, I mimic in my head, mirroring Jennifer's actions while partially obscured by the fountain spray. Maybe I should be happy Jean shoved me to the outskirts of every image, but if I'm participating in this photoshoot, I'd like to look pretty, at least—not a stiff, water-misted lump.

Is that too much to ask?

"You! Step back!" Jean yells at me.

Guess so.

AFTER ANOTHER DAY SPENT hustling around the lodge while Jean fawned over Jennifer and relegated me to the most unflattering of places—*okay, so I don't know how his photos will turn out, and I may be pleasantly surprised*—ice cream was in order.

Cherry chocolate chip, to be exact.

Hiking the grocery basket already filled with a bag of Munchies and Dr. Pepper into the crook of my elbow, I peruse the frozen aisle, searching for my favorite ice cream flavor.

"Vanilla, Rocky Road, Neapolitan..." *Where is it?* "Bingo!"

A pint of the sugary goodness bounces in the basket when someone tries reaching around me through the open freezer door. The rude guy doesn't acknowledge my presence except to push me aside to grab a gallon of vanilla.

"Excuse you," I mutter under my breath, and he finally spares a side glance before doing a double take as recognition lights his eyes.

"You're the fat chick from that show my girlfriend makes me watch every Wednesday. No wonder he hooked up with that other girl. She's fucking hot, and you're stuffing your face with junk."

A lot of words just spilled from this rude as hell *has no room to talk with his gallon of ice cream* jerk, and I feel bad for his poor girlfriend. From insulting my body to praising Hunter's decision to cheat on me, this guy deserves the lashing of the century, but my tongue refuses to work. A fierce rebuttal freezes in my throat.

Come on, Lauren! Stand up for yourself!

But nothing comes out.

Righteous anger swirls in my belly, but so does embarrassment and insecurity. This stranger pinpointed the best spots to launch an attack and landed each poisoned arrow with aplomb.

The bastard.

"What did you say to her?" A furious voice that decidedly does *not* belong to me enters the fray. The blast of heat suddenly at my back sends a thrill down my spine as my brain registers the familiar pissed tone. The same one used once I was escorted to his office after dousing him in coffee.

Ezra Caldwell.

The stern businessman I've ogled since the first time I saw his thick, muscular chest on display.

He's here.

Angry on my behalf.

Glancing up at my grumpy knight in shining armor, I bite my lip to hold back a sigh of pleasure. Late afternoon scruff covers his strong jawline, messing with his usual sleek put-togetherness, but instead of detracting from his handsomeness, it adds another layer of rugged beauty.

God, what is wrong with me?

I'm newly single and hiding from the tabloids. Even if a vacation fling was on the table, *which it certainly is not*, Ezra is off-limits. He owns the lodge I'm staying at. He's technically my boss as long as I'm modeling for his marketing campaign.

It's a bad idea all around.

Fucking Hunter.

My life was drama-free before him, and now it seems like life is laughing as it remedies the oversight—molding my future into one giant tangled mess with romance at the center.

CHAPTER THREE

EZRA

When Griffen called to see if I wanted to join him and Gramps on their weekly grocery trip, I jumped at the chance to get out of the office. The numbers on the computer screen were blurring together, and the comfort I usually found from burying myself in work was as elusive as a lodge vacancy on Valentine's Day—one of our busiest holidays, thanks to Suitor's Crossing's legend of *heart sparks*.

From a marketing standpoint, the fantasy of meeting your soulmate, or *heart spark*, at one of the town's romantic spots like the famous Suitor's Crossing Bridge or strolling our idyllic Main Street is a goldmine. It's great for business when tourists are eager to book a stay at Hearthstone Lodge with hopes of falling in love or affirming an established relationship.

In my opinion, however, it's a bunch of candy-coated bullshit.

The founding family that started the *heart spark* myth had enough business sense to spin the tale into a campaign for Suitor's Crossing. Refusing to let the town fade into obscurity like the many others that cropped up in the late 1800s during the state's few gold rushes.

I don't begrudge their savviness; I'm just too practical to fall for hearts and butterflies propaganda.

The same can't be said for the majority of town locals, including my sister.

"Something on your mind?" Gramps bumps my shoulder with his frailer one as we turn down the cereal aisle.

"Just work," I lie. It's not like me to zone out or dwell on something as trivial as *heart sparks*, but I know who to blame for the lapse: my meddling sister and a curvy songwriter. A quick internet search revealed exactly who Lauren Billingsley is and why she's hiding from the paparazzi.

Because of her asshole ex-boyfriend.

The realization that she's single shouldn't be branded into my brain, but I can't shake the unwanted thought.

"That's the only thing ever on your mind," Griffen says, dropping a box of Cheerios into the cart. "Between the lodge and your billion dollar hedge fund, it's no wonder Kennedy's cooked up her ridiculous scheme."

"Hang on. What scheme?"

Gramps and Griffen share a look before determinedly avoiding the question and wheeling into the next aisle full of frozen foods. A couple stands behind a frosted over freezer door, their conversation becoming clearer the closer we get.

"You're the fat chick from that show my girlfriend makes me watch every Wednesday," the man says. "No wonder he hooked up with that other girl. She's fucking hot, and you're stuffing your face with junk."

What the fuck?

A familiar beauty hits me square in the chest as I round the freezer door, prepared to lay into this jackass for speaking to a woman like that. But to discover he's talking to *Lauren* that way?

Fuck that shit.

"What did you say to her?" Instinctively, my arm circles her waist to place a protective hand on her soft belly. I read about the drama that went down on the reality show she participated in. About the lousy ex who cheated on her with a fellow housemate.

Righteous anger for her had swirled in my gut, but this douche wants to act like it's Lauren's fault?

"Who the hell are you?" His eyes dart behind me where I'm sure Gramps and Griffen have my back.

"Ezra Caldwell." Spend any time in Suitor's Crossing and you'll hear about the Caldwells and Hearthstone Lodge. I don't usually name drop, but there's no denying the satisfaction that hums in my veins the moment he recognizes who I am. "You owe this woman an apology."

He scoffs and tosses a container of ice cream in his cart with a clang. "For what? Telling the truth?"

"For being a misogynistic jerk who thinks it's okay to insult a woman in the middle of a goddamned grocery store." My temper rises, though I keep my tone at a respectable volume.

Glancing back at my family, I catch their surprised expressions.

Okay, mostly respectable.

"Ezra..." Lauren covers my hand on her stomach with her own. "I can handle this. I don't want a scene."

As if realizing he's got the makings of a solid payday in front of him, the man whips out his phone and snaps a picture before smirking. "Maybe Hunter had another reason to leave your fat ass. Maybe you were screwing around on him."

For the first time in my life, I black out.

That's the only reasonable explanation for why the gloating bastard is knocked out cold on the scuffed tile, and my fist hurts like a motherfucker.

"Holy shit." Griffen pounds my back with pride while Gramps walks over to nudge the man on the ground with the toe of his boot.

"One punch," Gramps drawls. "Didn't know you had it in you, kid. You were always the *fight with your words rather than fists* type. But he definitely deserved what he got."

"I can't believe... Y-you..." Lauren stutters in shock as I bend to grab the man's phone and quickly delete the photo he took. Even going so far as to permanently delete it from his trash. He won't receive a dime from the tabloids now.

"Breathe," I murmur, ushering her away from the scene of the crime, Gramps and Griffen hot on my heels.

I feel sorry for whoever finds the guy lying prone next to the Ben & Jerry's, but I'm not sticking around for when he wakes up. It's bad enough I punched him in the first place.

What the hell came over me?

"Lauren, this is my brother Griffen and our grandpa William." Both men wave in greeting.

"It's nice to meet you, although I'm sorry about the trouble."

"Don't worry about it. He had it coming for speaking to you that way." Griffen offers a modest grin and shrugs his big shoulders. All of the Caldwell men are large, but Griffen approaches giant-sized with his huge mitts and burly musculature. The irony is he's the most soft spoken of all of us. "Besides, it was worth seeing Ezra lose his cool."

My first instinct is to defend myself. I never lose my cool. But fuck if evidence to the contrary isn't still knocked out in aisle six.

"We're almost done here. Why don't you join us for dinner? I guarantee it'll brighten your evening," Gramps says.

"Oh, I wouldn't want to intrude."

"Nonsense. Ezra, be a gentleman and take the young lady's basket." Gramps offloads Lauren's basket into my quickly raised hand before ushering her toward the checkout lanes at the front of the store.

"Family dinner is going to be fun." Griffen hangs back with me as we slowly follow behind the pair. "Kennedy will love this."

"Speaking of our sister, you never told me about this scheme of hers." Maybe learning about Kennedy's machinations will distract me from staring at the sway of Lauren's hips and the bounce of her round ass.

Yeah, right.

"I thought it was obvious. She thinks you and Lauren should get together."

"Excuse me? I hardly know the woman." Except for the fact that she smells good enough to eat and those jeans do nothing to dispel an image of my palms cupping the peachy globes tempting me to take a bite.

"Yet you punched a man for insulting her. KO'ed with one shot. Gramps was right when he said it's not like you. You're the calm twin, while Beckett is the troublemaker."

I run a hand through my hair, disrupting the perfectly styled part I created this morning. "I barely remember doing it, though my knuckles ache like a bitch. Violence never pays," I mutter, disgruntled.

I wouldn't have made it far in business if I let my emotions rule so freely. That's why I keep a cool head. Plus, it's more satisfying to outmaneuver an opponent with strategy and logic rather than blunt force. Too bad some caveman part of my psyche decided to surface after thirty-some odd years.

Griffen unloads the cart of groceries onto the conveyor belt while Lauren and Gramps continue to chat. Their conversation is quiet, but every now and then, I catch my name sprinkled in with my siblings'.

Great, he's sharing our life story with her.

"Once we pay for this, you can use the frozen peas to soothe your hand." Griffen lowers his voice. "Unless you want Lauren to kiss it better."

"Shut up."

Lauren's lips are pink and plump and would feel amazing on my sore flesh, but I'm not getting tangled in whatever plan Kennedy's cooked up. She already forced me to allow Lauren to model for our next marketing campaign, meaning my office and the lodge have shrunk to a claustrophobic size when everywhere I turn Lauren is posing and showcasing her vibrant smile.

Dammit! I do not have time to obsess over a woman and think about her smile. Or her pretty violet eyes. Or the softness of her curves.

I'm not interested in a relationship; I'm too busy.

Kennedy knows this.

Hell, my entire family is aware.

Which will make tonight's weekly get-together a fucking minefield of pointed questions, knowing smirks, and trying like hell to avoid letting Lauren get caught in the crossfire. Because I doubt she's eager to date. She's fresh out of a relationship.

Sure, I'd treat her a thousand times better than her bastard ex, but it doesn't matter. We're not getting together. Kennedy and *heart sparks* be damned.

CHAPTER FOUR

LAUREN

The smell of garlic permeates the kitchen once Griffen removes the cheesy garlic bread from the oven. Somehow, I ended up in the Caldwell family home helping Ezra's brother cook dinner while their grandpa doctored Ezra's bruised hand.

Because he defended me.

Knocked that jerk on his ass.

It was insanely hot. Unexpected. Confusing as hell.

No one's ever protected me like that, and though I don't normally condone violence, I can't deny the immediate rush of heat that warmed my heart then settled between my thighs.

"Thanks for your help." Griffen sets the metal tray on a dish towel to cool as I chop vegetables for the dinner salad at the kitchen island.

"It's the least I can do."

"Since my uptight brother defended your honor?"

"Since who did what?" A tall, tattooed man swaggers into the kitchen looking remarkably like Ezra—in a disheveled, devil-may-care sort of way. Kennedy gave me the rundown of her brothers after that awkward meeting with Ezra and Jean Marcelle, which means this must be Ezra's firefighter twin.

"Some douche was harassing Lauren, so Ezra punched him out." Griffen mimes a fist to the jaw.

"You're kidding." The newcomer approaches me with a smile and offers his hand. "I'm Beckett, the levelheaded twin." He winks while holding onto my hand a second longer than necessary.

Kennedy had been right to warn me. Beckett is a flirt. An extremely attractive one. And if I were searching for a fling to help me forget about Hunter, he'd be the perfect choice—the bad boy fireman.

Too bad it's his grumpy brother my traitorous body reacts to. *Speak of the devil...*

Ezra enters the kitchen a second later, gauze wrapped around his injured hand—a scowl directed toward his brother's hold on my hand before I shake free—and settles on the bar seat beside me. His arm braces across the back of my chair while the other rests on the marble island, bracketing me with heat and causing a sliced cucumber to roll off the cutting board from a jolt of nerves.

"Careful, I don't want you accidentally cutting yourself." Ezra's large palm covers my knife-wielding hand before plucking the rogue cucumber off the counter and tossing it in his mouth. He tips his chin toward Beckett. "The only time you're levelheaded is in the middle of a fire, so don't even joke about coming for my title."

Beckett raises his hands in mock surrender, curiosity framing his features as he studies the two of us. "I'm not the one channeling Muhammad Ali in aisle six. When's your next match? I'll gather the crew for ringside support."

"Fuck off," Ezra says as he throws another cucumber slice at his brother's head. In a show of reflexes, Beckett catches and eats it in one smooth motion, and I bite my lip to keep from laughing.

It's nice being around the Caldwells.

I'm an only child borne of only children, so family time always consisted of a small trio. Visits to my grandparents were sporadic, since they lived in different parts of the country, and while my parents and I get along, we've never embodied the *Full House* chaos that currently streams through the air.

Beckett and Ezra teasing each other.

Griffen focusing on the final touches for dinner while staying out of the line of fire between his brothers.

When we move to the dining room, the comfortable jibing between siblings continues—Kennedy and their eldest brother Soren added to the mix—their grandpa, Soren's daughter, and Kennedy's partner jumping in whenever. I like how open they are with each other and how welcoming they are to me.

I almost forget why I'm here in the first place.

Because of that jerk at the store. Because of my escape from the spotlight back home.

"Everything okay? I know they're a lot, but they mean well." Ezra insisted on escorting me to my car after dinner, though it's not really necessary. I'm parked in the driveway on a well-lit cul de sac. I doubt there's much danger within the twenty feet between the front door and my vehicle.

"I'm fine. Your family is great."

"Even with all the questions?" he pushes.

Everyone was eager to ask about songwriting and what it's like working in the music industry. Who I've met. If they'd recognize any of my songs. It was sweet and reminded me of my love for music.

For a moment, Hunter had crushed my creativity—it's hard to write love songs when your heart's been stomped on—but some of my best work happened before I even met Hunter and we began writing together. Somehow, I'd forgotten that.

Songwriting, Hunter, and freaking *Harmony House* had become so intertwined that it seemed impossible to think about one thing without the others. The Caldwells' innocent questions made me realize that's not true. Music, the art of creating, transcends just one person or dramatic event.

"Even with all the questions," I assure him. The headlights flash when I unlock my car, and Ezra swoops in to open the driver's side door for me, the bright white of the gauze around his knuckles shining in the evening shadows.

"Thanks again for earlier. You didn't have to step in, but I appreciate it, and dinner was lovely." I'm rambling, suddenly nervous, as I gesture to his hand and the house behind him.

We're alone for the first time. No Caldwells as a buffer. No Hearthstone Lodge employees to run interference.

Completely alone except for the flutter of curtains at my periphery indicating we might have an audience, after all. Something my brain happily ignores when it decides to make everything ten times more awkward by directing my fingers to grasp his shoulder, lift up on my toes, and press a kiss to Ezra's stubbled cheek like it's the most natural thing in the world.

Oh my god, what the hell am I doing?

My heels slap against the pavement. Shaky hand falls to my side.

"I'm sorry. I don't know what—"

A frustrated growl rents the air before Ezra devours the apology with a firm kiss to my lips, his palm cupping the back of my head as I stumble backward into the cool metal of my car.

"Don't fucking apologize," he grumbles, ending the kiss with a harsh groan. A wild gleam shimmers in his dark eyes. "Maybe Beckett has a point. Maybe I'm not so levelheaded anymore. You fuck with my control, Lauren."

"Sorry...?" I'm not sure if it's a good or bad thing, especially when my hormones are shouting that it's an excellent thing, desperate to experience more of his passionate fervor.

"Stop. Apologizing." He nips at my bottom lip before licking the sting away. "It just means I need to readjust my thinking on some things. *On you.*" His fingers playfully tug on the end of my ponytail, then he steps back to let me bonelessly sink into my car.

With a tap on the window, his low gravel-toned voice swaddles me with a warm "Goodnight, Lauren. I'll see you soon" as I back out of the drive and leave him in my rearview mirror—the ache he ignited in my blood sure to keep me up for the rest of the night.

CHAPTER FIVE

EZRA

I kissed Lauren.

She thanked me for dealing with that asshole at the store with an innocent peck to my cheek, then my dick pushed for more. All evening, I'd battled the raging erection straining against my thigh as Lauren fit in perfectly with my family, and the moment she gave me an opening—outside Griffen and Gramps's home for fuck's sake—I stole more than a peck from her very sweet and very kissable lips.

The Caldwell Clan had a field day with that one. Teasing me mercilessly the second I reentered the house.

What the fuck is wrong with me?

She's technically an employee—even though she refused to sign a contract and earn a paycheck, relabeling it as a goodwill gesture after our initial *coffee to the head* meet-cute.

And she's definitely a lodge guest.

Both of those things mean it'd be out of bounds to pursue her further, and I always stay within the bounds of propriety for business and my personal life. They never mix.

"Did you see that Jean emailed the first batch of images?" Kennedy pops through my office doorway the next morning.

"He did?" I click around on my computer and open the attached folder of raw photos. "Come take a look; I've got it open now."

She rounds my desk to hover over my shoulder as I scroll through the files of Jennifer Q and Lauren, and the more I see, the angrier I get.

"What the fuck?"

"Is that all of them?" The concern in Kennedy's voice matches my frustration. Clearly, we noticed the same problem.

"Yeah, that's the entire folder."

A folder full of images that almost seem malicious in intent because Lauren is relegated to the background in every single one. The angles and lighting are off, and while her natural beauty prevents the photos from being totally unusable, it doesn't take an expert to see how Jean spent effort bringing out the best in Jennifer while ignoring Lauren.

Grabbing the phone receiver, I press '1' for my assistant. "Could you find Jean Marcelle and bring him to my office, please?"

Kennedy waits until I hang up before asking, "What are you going to do?" She sits in one of the chairs across from my desk and crosses her legs.

"I'm going to find out why he's wasting our time and money and insulting Lauren at the same time. Depending on his answer, I might fire him."

"Sounds reasonable. Especially since he completely ignored the brief. We specifically wanted Lauren highlighted due to her current celebrity status."

"Instead, we got the Jean and Jennifer show. I knew we should have hired Kent Moreland." Kent is a world renowned photographer who moved to Suitor's Crossing a few years ago. He's worked with us in the past, so I know I can trust his work.

"Sorry..." Kennedy squirms in her seat. "This is my fault. I pushed for Jean, and look what happened."

"It's not on you. I vetted him as well. You think I'd hire someone without checking their portfolio? His previous work is good."

"With models like Jennifer Q."

Surprised by my sister's insinuation, I start, "Lauren may not be a professional but—"

"That's not what I'm referring to. Do you remember when I was obsessed with watching *Project Runway* reruns?"

I groan and lean back in my chair. "How could I forget? You made 'make it work' your catchphrase for a year."

She smiles and shrugs. "Yeah, well, most of those designers failed at the challenges where they had to work with real women. They either had no clue what to do with someone over a size zero or outright sneered at fitting plus-sized clients. Maybe Jean is one of those."

"Are you serious?" Lauren is gorgeous, no matter her size, though as far as I'm concerned her lush curves are a delicious bonus. "He's definitely getting fired."

"I don't know for sure that's what's going on," she huffs with a roll of her eyes. "It's just a possibility. And I know you like Lauren, but try to keep your cool when he gets here."

"I don't like Lauren, at least, not in the way you're suggesting."

"Oh? Did I imagine you kissing her after yesterday's dinner?"

Avoiding eye contact, I stare at the door, waiting for Jean Marcelle's arrival. "You shouldn't be spying."

Her expression of denial gets interrupted when my assistant appears with Jean.

"Take a seat. We were reviewing the email you sent and have some questions." I wait for the man to settle beside Kennedy then jump straight to the point. "We're disappointed by the lack of attention to Lauren. We expressed our desire for her to take center stage in this campaign, so why have you ignored our wishes?"

Jean clasps his hands in his lap. Disdain wrinkles his nose. "Respectfully, *monsieur*, but Miss Lauren doesn't possess the qualities needed for your campaign. She's not photogenic and—"

"Excuse me?" I boom, my ire rising to new heights at the blatant disgust in his tone. *So much for keeping my cool.* "She's extremely photogenic. A young, beautiful woman. What I'm hearing is that you are not talented enough to recognize the prize you have in front of you. Nor do you possess the skill required for this job. With that said, you're fired. Effective immediately."

Jean splutters in disbelief while my sister covers a cough of shocked amusement. I won't tolerate anyone insulting Lauren. First the douche at the grocery store and now this pompous photographer? Not on my watch.

"You can't fire me. We have a contract!"

"Which gives me the right to terminate our working relationship if at any time Hearthstone Lodge's best interests are in jeopardy. A contracted employee who willfully defies strict orders for the final product falls within those boundaries. You may see yourself out."

A flurry of French explodes from Marcelle as he stomps out of the room. He can curse me all he wants; he's the one who fucked up and lost a contract with the Pacific Northwest's premier mountain resort.

"Nicely done." Kennedy applauds with a knowing smirk twisting the corner of her mouth. "Let's hope Kent Moreland is free to step in. I'll call Nora to explain what happened with Jean. I'm sure she didn't know he'd be so size-ist when that's against everything she promotes."

One click of my mouse sends the email inquiry to Kent about taking over the campaign photoshoot, then I stand and straighten my jacket. "I'll find Lauren. She kept how badly Marcelle was treating her to herself."

"Don't be too hard on her," she says, following me out the door.

I grunt in response.

My phone buzzes with a message from security answering my question on Lauren's whereabouts. I don't often request the location of guests, but everything about our celebrity resident has me acting in ways I never have before.

Punching people.

Yelling at them.

It's like she's snipped at the strands that bind my control, unleashing every fiery emotion I've spent years subduing in order to succeed as a cold, logical businessman.

I don't like it.

It makes for bad business decisions when a man runs on something as fickle as feelings.

I loathe it.

And Lauren's about to find out how much.

CHAPTER SIX

LAUREN

"Miss Billingsley." The icy blast from Ezra sends a chill down my spine. From the formality of my last name to his glacial stare, I'm guessing he spent the night remembering why our kiss never should have happened rather than indulging in some *self-care* at the memory.

"Mr. Caldwell." I match his serious tone and cautiously rise from my spot leaning against the pillar where Jennifer Q and I have met Jean Marcelle every morning this week. He's late, but that's the least of my worries with Mr. Tall, Dark, and Cloudy bearing down on me.

"Lauren! There are rumors that Hunter is searching for you. Are you ignoring his calls?" Bright flashing lights blind me for a moment. The ambush is unexpected considering the lodge's increased security since my arrival, but paparazzi are like cockroaches—no matter how many you kill, one always pops up to replace it.

"Fuck, Jennifer handle this," Ezra instructs the supermodel next to me, who eagerly rushes to intercept the photogs heading our way. His hand takes mine and ushers me across the gleaming marble floor and down multiple hallways before pulling me into a supply closet. The door shuts behind us with a soft snick, a blanket of ominous silence settling over our shoulders.

"I'm sorry. This is like a never-ending apology tour," I weakly joke. A sliver of light peeks under the door. Otherwise, darkness shrouds us in shadows while the smell of chemical cleaners permeates the air.

"Well, this time it should be me apologizing to you. This is my property. My security should be doing a better job of protecting you from those bloodsuckers."

"They can't be everywhere one hundred percent of the time," I point out, not wanting any of his employees to get into trouble because of me.

"That's what cameras are for. Twenty-four-seven coverage."

Gingerly relaxing against a shelving unit, I sigh. "I wish they'd forget about me already. The show's finale aired already. Another scandal should distract them soon."

"What about you? Could *you* use a distraction?" A huskiness enters his voice as his fingers caress my cheek.

My breath stutters in my lungs. I figured our kiss was a one-off, especially based on how he acted earlier, but maybe I was wrong.

God, let me be wrong.

"What kind of distraction?"

"The orgasmic kind." His lips brush across mine then retreat. "Is that okay?"

"It depends. What changed between you calling me *Miss Billingsley* out there and now? Aside from the mad dash to escape the paparazzi."

"I was angry, but not at you. I fired Jean Marcelle this morning because of the horrible way he was treating you," he admits. "When I think of you, I lose all semblance of control, and lately, you're all I think about. That's not good for business, Lauren."

Another apology is on the tip of my tongue, but I swallow it in favor of a question. "What do you mean you fired Marcelle because of me?"

"He purposely set out to make you look bad, not that he had a prayer of succeeding. You're too damn gorgeous." Ezra's roughened fingertips trace down my cheek to my throat, pausing at the rapid pulse of my heartbeat. "He insulted you, so he had to go. I was coming to find you to share the news and find out how far his abuse went when we got sidetracked."

"Don't worry, he never said much to me. Jennifer was his focus." And I figured she'd be Ezra's too, but it sounds like he wanted me front and center. Kennedy had pushed for me to do the shoot to garner interest from the public because of my current popularity, but he'd never seemed on board with the notion.

I thought he was appeasing his sister.

But he just fired a famous photographer because he treated me poorly.

Butterflies take flight in my belly as I sink my hands into his hair, tunneling through the styled strands.

"Okay." I nod to answer his previous question then remember he can't see me too well in the dark. "Distract me, Ezra."

He claims my mouth with a harsh groan, bumping me backward and causing a couple of cleaning bottles to wobble next to my head. This close, his spicy cologne masks the strong odor of bleach and ammonia, and I almost laugh at our terrible timing.

Sex in a supply closet? Not the most romantic place at Hearthstone Lodge, but it'll do in a pinch. *Or when you're on the run from paparazzi hounds.*

Eager hands toy with the hem of my shirt before dipping beneath and skimming my belly to cup my breasts. "I can't wait to taste these beauties," he rasps. "So soft and heavy, overflowing my palms. I just know your nipples are going to taste like ripe little cherries."

A whimper escapes my throat, and I release my hold on him, frantically whipping my top off and shimmying my bra down my arms to free my breasts. Immediately, the sensitive tips tighten, ready for the wet warmth of Ezra's lips suckling the tender flesh.

"Why don't you find out?" I dare, a previously unknown sexual goddess slinking to the forefront.

With a growl, Ezra drops lower to trail kisses across my cheek, neck, and collarbone before wrapping his lips around one nipple and sucking hard. I jump at the forceful contact, a hint of pain morphing into pleasure. The sharp edges of his teeth scrape along the areola to hold the engorged tip for the lashing of his tongue.

"Ezra..." My thighs rub together in search of relief as I arch my back. Desperate to shove deeper into the hot cavern of his mouth.

"Cherries, just like I thought. Does this pussy taste the same, you think?" My jeans are swiftly unbuttoned and jerked down my legs along with my panties until they tangle around my knees.

Two fingers slip between my soaking folds, glide past my clit, and plunge into my aching channel. A muted moan clogs my throat. It feels so good, but I know he's only just beginning. And when his cock fills me... My eyes roll toward the ceiling, shuddering in anticipation.

"Please..."

My other nipple receives the same punishing treatment as the first one before Ezra sinks to his knees. His tongue paints a wet path from my chest to my navel, dipping into my belly button, following the crease of my thigh.

"Fuck, I can smell how aroused you are, baby. You're dripping at the thought me tongue-fucking this tight little pussy."

Damn, for an uptight businessman, Ezra sure does have a filthy mouth.

And I fucking love it.

CHAPTER SEVEN

EZRA

When those paparazzi bastards appeared, I'd wanted to fight every single one of them off. Smash their cameras and warn them away from Lauren.

Of course, that's crazy behavior and would only add fuel to the fire, so I did the next best thing. I got Lauren the hell away from them.

To a damn supply closet.

My *newly favorite* supply closet because I'm on my knees about to eat her pussy like a starving man as my thumbs spread her slick folds.

I wish I could see better, but the damn lighting in here sucks. There's probably a light switch or a string hanging from a bulb overhead, but I'm not wasting time now when I'm so close to what I want.

Burying my face between her warm thighs, the first lick elicits a high-pitched squeak from Lauren. The second a groan of pleasure.

"Goddamn, baby. I didn't think you could get any sweeter, but this pussy... You're gonna spread for me every day, aren't you? Let me tongue your hard little clit and suck these pussy lips?"

Lauren pants in approval, her nails digging into my shoulders, as I perform each action with a flourish, alternating between licks and sucks, savoring her unique honeyed flavor, until she comes with a short scream.

"Perfect. Gorgeous," I praise while petting her trembling curves.

After the last of her orgasm fades, I rise to my feet and kiss her with glossy lips. She hungrily lets me in, sucking on my tongue and moaning.

"Such a dirty girl. You love tasting yourself on my tongue, don't you?"

"I love kissing you," she admits.

"Good thing I plan on doing it for a long, long time." It's the closest I've ever been to voicing a commitment, which should freak me the fuck out.

My control is already frayed around Lauren. Allowing her closer will only mean more fraying, more chaotic and confusing feelings. But something stops me from pulling away.

Like she's the sun, and I'm caught in her orbit.

Damn, maybe Kennedy's belief in heart sparks *isn't as far-fetched as I believed.*

THE CROSSING GUARD waves me forward after a line of kids passes in front of my niece's elementary school. Normally, my brother Soren would be on pick up duty, but I promised to do it after he texted that his tour was running long. As the lodge's resident outdoorsman, Soren handles the more rigorous guest activities like leading groups on horseback through mountain trails.

"Hey, Uncle Ezra!" Sara Beth tosses her backpack onto the backseat then buckles into place beside it.

I flip on the turn signal and wait before merging into the slow-crawling school pick-up line. "How was school? Anything interesting happen?"

"We learned about food chains. Poor Whiskers is near the bottom." She grimaces at the thought of her fluffy white bunny being some predator's dinner.

"Lucky for you and Whiskers he's safe at home, hmm? He's living a life of luxury." Spoiled by his young caretaker.

Sara Beth smiles, revealing another tooth missing from her upper teeth, before babbling about other animals and their place on nature's food chain until I pull into the lodge parking lot.

"What's going on over there?" She points toward a circle of vans and a horde of people with cameras—and not just DSLRs. They've got larger filming cameras set on their shoulders.

What the hell?

The crowd seems centered around one man who's leading the pack down a path that leads to the back of the lodge. Parking in a spot near the side entrance closest to my office, I help Sara Beth from the car, my focus split.

"Let's get you settled, then I'll find out who they are," I say, hurrying her inside.

I have a sinking feeling that I know exactly what they're doing here—waiting to harass Lauren.

We're meeting for coffee, although a little later than originally planned because of Soren and Sara Beth. Did someone send in a tip to the tabloids? Is she expecting me to appear only to be ambushed?

Texting my head of security, I order him to gather a few men and meet me behind the lodge. We'll need a small army to waylay the sea of press, but what's the use of being a billionaire, if I can't use my money to pay for top notch security and protect my woman?

My feet freeze on the pavement.

My woman?

"Uncle Ezra? What's wrong?"

Oh, nothing, kid. I just had a life-altering epiphany. But that's not something you share with ten year old nieces, so I cobble together a lame excuse for my pause, secure her in my office, then rush back outside.

I quickly retrace the path of the camera crews as adrenaline spikes in my veins. Fuck, I *want* Lauren. She's *mine*. Feelings of possessiveness mix with a need to protect her, and they buoy my stride to a light jog.

I'm afraid I won't find her before the press, but I damn well plan on becoming her shield when I do. Because she's done being plagued by these vultures.

If they want a piece of Lauren, they'll have to go through me first, and anyone familiar with Ezra Caldwell will tell them: *I'm a tough son of a bitch.*

CHAPTER EIGHT

LAUREN

The afternoon sunlight warms my shoulders as I relax in one of the Adirondack chairs scattered on the stone patio outside the lodge. It's set up in tiers that weave through a garden of dormant shrubs and bare trees. In the spring, I'm sure it's beautiful, but the stark winter visage holds its own kind of wonder, too.

Ezra messaged earlier to postpone our coffee date, mentioning needing to pick up his niece from school. It's sweet how involved he is. My extended family didn't live anywhere near me while growing up, which made impromptu pick-ups impossible. Plus, I took the bus since my parents worked during that time.

"Lauren. Lauren!"

The sip of my latte spews from my lips at the sound of my name in that overly friendly tone.

Oh, no.

My metal chair scrapes across the stone as I stand, fighting to regain my equilibrium.

Hunter is here, and he brought an entourage.

A smug grin plasters his face before he tugs me into an awkward hug. "There you are! Do you know how hard I've been trying to reach you? *Harmony House* wants us back for a reunion show."

Hunter's audacity remains unmatched. How dare he track me down and suggest I'd ever want to work with him again? As if I'd want to appear on a reunion show with him and Mya, who last I heard was still fucking my ex.

"Are you out of your mind? I'm not filming a reunion show." The end of my ponytail stings my eye because my head shakes *no* so fast. "I'm never doing reality TV again."

"Come on, Lo. Don't be like that," he whines. *Ugh, I can't believe I used to date this wheedling jerk.* "Our storyline made ratings history for the network. Imagine how well a live reunion will do! You, me, Mya... It's a guaranteed hit."

"It's a guaranteed trainwreck. You humiliated me in front of millions of people, and you never even apologized. Now, you expect me to prostrate myself for the public again?"

"That's what this is about? An apology?" He runs a hand through his shaggy hair. "I wanted to do it right. There's a whole thing planned for the reunion, but if you need to hear it now, I'm sorry, okay?"

"No, not okay. Take your fake apology and shove it up your ass. I came to Suitor's Crossing to get away from you and the tabloids, and you're screwing that up by bringing them to witness whatever this is." I gesture between us.

A group of photogs are crowded at the edges of the stone patio, snapping shot after shot like their lives depend on capturing Hunter and I in the throes of an argument.

"Everything all right here?" Ezra's familiar voice enters the fray, and I'm torn between being happy he's here and embarrassed that he's getting another glimpse at how much of a mess my life's been lately.

"Everything's cool, man. Just a little spat with my girl. You know how it is." Hunter offers an affable smile.

"I'm not your girl."

"She's not your girl."

Hunter looks between me and Ezra, his brows furrowing as confusion wipes away some of his earlier charm.

"If you're not a guest of Hearthstone Lodge, then you're not welcome on our property, and it's considered trespassing. Do I need to get Sheriff Lawson here?"

"Whoa, easy... There's no need for the cops. Lauren, tell this guy who I am."

"I know who you are," Ezra growls. "You're the asshole who couldn't keep his dick in his pants. Who thought another woman could replace Lauren. Who fucked up and lost the best thing you'll never have again."

Wow, Ezra is freaking hot when he's defending me, and Hunter's expression of annoyed disbelief is just the cherry on top. He thought he could show up and bully me into doing what he wanted like when he first asked me to join *Harmony House*.

Think again, loser.

"Lauren..."

"Don't speak to her. Don't ever say her name again." Ezra's large body forms a barrier between me and Hunter. "I'm going to count to ten, if you're not out of my sight and off my property in that time, then those paparazzi friends of yours are going to get a camera full of your face looking a hell of a lot less pretty after my fist breaks your nose."

Hunter huffs and acts like he's going to push, but a glance at the cameras has him changing his mind.

"Fine, I'll go, but think about the offer, okay, babe?"

I don't bother answering him. I'm just happy when he finally leaves.

"That's going to air on E! tonight," I mumble, my palm hesitantly rubbing circles over Ezra's tense back.

His head of security arrives with a host of men in black, who herd the cameramen off the property. Once the excitement has died down, the guests who stopped to witness our debacle move on, and Ezra guides me inside the lodge.

He silently punches the button for the elevator and selects my level.

Guess we're going to my room to talk this out.

Does he think I'm more trouble than I'm worth?

He probably isn't used to dealing with D-list celebrities traipsing around his property and causing problems. And I'm just a guest. It's not like I permanently live here, even if the thought of moving to this small town has grown on me the past week.

Especially since Nashville doesn't feel safe anymore with Hunter, Mya, and their slew of cameras.

My room door unlocks with the tap of Ezra's phone, and soon we're locked in privacy—the weight of our relationship's future burdening my shoulders.

I open my mouth to apologize. "I'm sorry for—"

He shuts me up with a possessive kiss that steals my breath away. "No more apologies. No more talking about your ex." He punctuates the statement by tearing off my knitted wrap dress, leaving me bare except for my bra and panties.

"But..." He doesn't want an explanation for what happened? For Hunter's visit?

Rippling muscles snag my attention as Ezra unbuttons his shirt. His abdomen flexes, and my gaze follows the enticing vee that leads to the thick bulge in his pants.

"But *nothing*, Lauren, and if you disobey me, there will be consequences." Leather loafers fly through the air. Black slacks slump to the carpet.

"Like what?"

The more Ezra uncovers, the less I care about the last fifteen minutes. Hunter is gone, thanks to the dominant billionaire currently standing naked in front of me, so why dwell on the past?

Ezra stalks forward, his cock swaying between his muscular thighs, and I lick my suddenly dry lips. For a man who sits behind a desk most days, he's incredibly fit—the complete opposite of my squishy curves.

"Like my palm staining your pretty ass red with my handprint," he warns with a feral smirk stretching across his face. "Like my cock ramming so deep in your tight pussy that you'll forget about every man before me."

"That's a confident claim. Are you sure you can live up to it?" The taunt spills forth without preamble, announcing the arrival of my inner sex goddess awakening again.

There's no doubt in my mind that Ezra has the skills to scramble my brain and have my pussy aching for more—our interlude in the supply closet proved that—but a part of me wants him to show me just how much he wants me.

He says I break his control?

Well, I want to see it in all its growly glory.

Quicker than the snap of a camera, Ezra pins me to the solid dresser next to the window that overlooks the mountains on the horizon. His larger body cages me against the dark-stained wood and guides my hands to the top for support as the rectangular mirror attached to the dresser reflects our flushed forms.

"Naughty little tease," he whispers in my ear before biting the lobe. "Just for that, I'm going to make you forget your own name. All you'll be screaming is mine for the entire lodge to hear."

A shiver works its way down my exposed skin, though I'm far from cold. I'm burning up from the inside out with the furnace that is Ezra Caldwell at my back, the hot ridge of his cock wedged between my ass cheeks.

"Promises, promises..." The provoking words are barely spoken when the flat of his hand lands on my bottom with a resounding crack. I jump at the unexpected contact and wiggle against the wall of muscle preventing me from avoiding another spanking.

Not that I truly want to dodge Ezra's erotic discipline, but it's difficult to keep still when you're desperate for release.

His finger slips beneath the top of my panties and tugs the fabric higher until the wet cloth binds my clit in a tight embrace while the rest of the cotton lewdly rubs my back hole.

Oh, fuck. Ezra's barely begun his onslaught, yet I'm already shaking, panting with desire and nerves because no one's ever made me feel this aroused this fast.

My bra snaps open and falls forward, freeing my breasts for his sensual pinches then soothing caresses, drawing my nipples into throbbing reddened points.

"Ezra... Please..."

"That's a good start, baby. Beg me. Moan my name." He pulls on my panties again as the broad tip of his cock nestles between my soaked folds, and the dual sensation of cotton and hard male teasing my entrance forces my spine to hollow, driving my pussy back for more.

Until, finally, his mushroom head stretches the clenching muscles, shoving my panties to the side.

"I'm going to fuck you so good." Another thick inch slides forward. "I'm going to fuck this sweet cunt, and you're going to watch." More cock, more stretching. *God, he's torturing me.* "Watch these sexy tits bounce with each thrust. Watch me mark your pretty body with my teeth." A bite to my shoulder before sucking the pain away to leave behind his claim.

I'm surrounded by Ezra. Completely at his mercy.

Yet I've never felt more powerful.

Gone is the uptight businessman who maintains fastidious control of his life. In his place is this wild beast devouring me whole with savage obsession.

The passionate choreography outlined in the mirror showcases Ezra's undeniable virility and dominance as he buries himself deep again and again, my body accepting each heavy thrust eagerly.

"Yes, mark me. Use me. Make me yours," I ramble, jolting from the milking of my clit and nipple in time with the vigorous pounding of my pussy.

"You're already mine, Lauren," he grunts.

Oh, wow...

My mouth falls open with the scream of his name, and I come hard, blinding stars bursting behind my eyelids as I shudder and moan, grasping for purchase on Ezra's sturdy forearms.

"That's it, baby. Let everyone know who you belong to." His movements become less controlled, more erratic, until he roars his release, hot jets of his seed overflowing from where we're joined.

Good thing I'm on the pill, I think dazedly.

We stand locked together for long moments. Our breathing syncing. Our hearts matching beat for beat.

A small giggle erupts from my chest as I take in our sweaty appearance.

"What's so funny?" Ezra nuzzles the space between my neck and shoulder, clearly one earth shattering orgasm eased the furious beast he turned into the second we entered my hotel room.

"Us. Like this." I tiredly nod toward the mirror. My ponytail has half fallen out. My bra hangs wrinkled and crushed between me and the dresser, while Ezra's usually styled hair clings to his temples and forehead, a sweaty mess from my fingers reaching back to grab on at some point. "We're a mess."

Ezra studies our entwined bodies then shrugs. "I like it."

"Me, too... So would the paparazzi. I can see the headline: *Humiliated Songwriter Gets Even with Billionaire*."

"I could arrange for that, you know. Rub Hunter's face in how badly he fucked up." He pauses and retreats enough to meet my eyes. "How are you feeling about seeing him again?"

"I'm allowed to talk about my ex now?" I tease.

"With my cum dripping down your thighs? Sure." A satisfied grin tips his lips, male pride emanating from him.

Resting my head on his pec, I sigh. "His appearance shocked me, but that's about it. I'm not harboring an unrequited love for him, more like unrequited loathing. I can't believe he thinks I'd want to do a reunion show with him."

"That's what his visit was about? What a jackass."

"Right?" Spinning in his embrace, Ezra's cock falls from my pussy, and we both groan at the sensation before I forge ahead, ignoring the kindling need to be taken by him again. "I just hope he takes the hint and leaves me alone from now on."

"If he doesn't, he'll have me to deal with."

Warmth settles in my chest at the firm assurance. I pat his chest then press a kiss over his heart. "Of course he will. You're my knight in shining armor, aren't you? The guy in the grocery store. Jean Marcelle."

"I'll always protect you," he confirms, and despite our short time together, I believe him.

I trust Ezra.

And for the first time since *Harmony House* and Hunter, I feel hopeful for the future with my gruff protector at my side.

EPILOGUE

EZRA

SIX MONTHS LATER

"These look amazing!" Lauren fawns over the finished marketing materials set to release in a few months for next spring's campaign. Though the crazed interest in her has dimmed since multiple celebrity scandals have cropped up recently, we chose to keep Lauren as our primary model anyway—she's gorgeous, I love her, and I couldn't care less about her influencer status, so it was a no-brainer.

"Kent did an excellent job," I agree from behind her, pressing a kiss to the back of her neck. Glossy brochures and posters are spread out on the conference table waiting for my final approval, but honestly, if Lauren's happy then so am I.

"I guess if songwriting ever fails me, modeling can be my backup plan," she jokes as if she wasn't just nominated for a music award.

In between dates around Suitor's Crossing and sex around the lodge and my cabin, Lauren scribbled a notebook full of new lyrics that eventually turned into three major hits for a popular country singer and one song promises to become an awards show darling.

"What if I have a better backup plan?"

She turns in my arms with a hum of curiosity, and a rash of nerves surges through me. This isn't how I wanted to do this; I'd imagined whisking Lauren to Paris and romancing her with wine and chocolate, but the opportunity to know her answer now is too much to resist.

"What are you talking about?" she asks, tilting her head to the side.

Reaching into the inside pocket of my jacket, I retrieve the small velvet box I've kept close to my heart for the past month. It pops open with a soft click that Lauren's surprised gasp quickly masks.

"I'm talking about the future. Marriage." I drag a labored breath through my lungs. We've discussed our dreams of family and forever, but we never set a timeline. Six months ago, we barely knew each other, but this is Suitor's Crossing—a town built on *heart sparks*, soulmates—and Lauren is mine.

Ignoring the slight tremble in my hand, I offer the ring to her, my heart literally in my hand. "I love you, Lauren Elaine soon-to-be Caldwell, I hope. From your unbelievable violet eyes to your sexy curves. From your immense talent to your kind heart. You've stolen all of my control, broken the boundaries I put on myself, and freed me to a life of love. Please say you'll be my wife."

Tears drip down her cheeks. The glossy sheen over her extraordinary purple gaze highlights the specks of deeper lavender buried within.

Is it normal for a woman to cry at a marriage proposal?

Lauren cups my cheeks and smiles, giving me hope that I haven't totally fucked this up. "Yes, I'll be your wife, Ezra." She levers herself high enough to seal the promise with a kiss. "You're my protector, my love. *My muse.* And my life wouldn't be complete without you."

"Thank fuck," I groan.

Sweeping a hand across the table to toss all the papers to the floor, I lift my woman in my arms and set her on the cleared wood top. The ring easily slides onto her left hand, and I kiss the spot before showing my new fiancée exactly how much she means to me.

Something the whole of Hearthstone Lodge learns, too.